Marco A

TRAIN YOUR DOG
WATCHING A VIDEO!

AmDogTraining Adventure

ISBN Code: 9798786984003

Learn how to look at the world

through your dog's eyes

AmDogTraining

Preface

We all wish we were Olivia

I only had to watch one video-tutorial on his YouTube channel AmDogTraining to realise that Marco would go a very long way. His tutorials can be watched for free, and are very intuitive, clear and deliver lots of advice due to years of experience, his genuine love of dogs and deep knowledge concerning issues that people face when adopting a dog. Marco's goal is to provide dog adopters with the best tips to build up and strengthen their relationship with their four-legged friend. The videos, masterfully edited by Nicola Atzori, are "work in progress" because new videos become available based on requests, questions, and new ideas.

Marco is truly an expert: he is an Agility and ENCI's (equivalent of the Kennel Club in Italy) judge, a columnist for the Italian magazine Quattro Zampe, a lecturer on dog behaviour and is regularly invited to speak on radio and TV shows. Now he is also a writer thanks to his first book, which will certainly be a great success.

Marco has also involved his children in his training activity: Emanuele, who is only 14 years old, is already a video maker for AmDogTraining and is aspiring to improve his skills in the world of the web.

What can I say about sweet Olivia? The new arrival, a beautiful Flat Coated Retriever, who has become an inspiration and a guide for many of us, protagonist of countless video tutorials which represent a virtual encyclopedia on how to manage your dog, from puppy to adult, whose ethological needs are fully understood and fulfilled by someone who is entirely dedicated to understanding man's best friend. Thank you, Marco, for your useful and constructive social function.

Maria Paola Gianni
Head of Quattro Zampe magazine

Instructions

Before you start reading the following pages, I'd like to give you some helpful tips.

The book is divided into three different sections to make it clear and practical. You'll easily find what you need as the different segments are clearly pointed out in the margin.

In the first section I wanted to explain the journey I took which brought me to a new way of seeing things, moving towards cynophilia and leaving behind anthropocentrism in dog training. The goal is the well-being of both dog and adopter and it is achieved through a clear method, commitment, knowledge and a lot of respect for our four-legged friends.

New technology is extremely helpful as videos help me to show you how to train your dog using my method and they explain in detail the various situations you may face and how to deal with them. You can find my tutorials on YouTube and on the AmDogTraining website which you can watch as many times as you like.

The main goal is to improve your relationship with your four-legged friend and give you the ability to train your dog independently.

All of this has been possible thanks to Nicola Atzori, whose computer skills, patience and support have been fundamental in the creation of this book and the AmDogTraining website.

In the second part of the book you can find a range of information that is really important for your everyday life with both puppies and adult dogs.

The book ends with a final section dedicated to a series of *"Goals - activities"*.

Important: In each chapter you will find several QR codes, which will take you to links, videos or playlists on AmDogTraining's YouTube channel, which is very dynamic and constantly updated with new tutorials.

The *AmDogTraining adventure* has just begun!

Part one

Nothing is constant,
but change!
(Buddha - Siddhārtha Gautama Shakyamuni)

My dogs

I walked into my friend's shop already knowing what to ask for. But my eyes wandered to the collars, leashes, bags of dog food, and bowls of all shapes and sizes. Finally my friend freed herself from her customers and came towards me.

"Do you by any chance have two parakeets?" I asked her bluntly. She shook her head. As I imagined, she would have to order them, but fate had something else in store for me.

She told me that at home she had a boxer puppy, barely four months old, which she had not been able to sell. She couldn't take me to see her, as the shop was open, but she suggested that I popped in on my own to have a look.

"If you like her, she's yours!" She handed me the keys, which I grabbed and shortly after I was standing in front of the little boxer: she was brindled, with a lovely expression, but rather thin. If I'm honest I would have called her an ugly dog.

I was in my early twenties and had already had two dogs in my life: Kettor, a mixed pinscher, and Spank, another mixed breed.

That same day I took America, this was the boxer puppy's name which would later become Emi, home instead of the parakeets.

Soon I realised that I was having difficulties in managing my puppy, who was having issues with socialisation. Even a simple walk could become a worry.

I enrolled in a dog training course.

At that time dog training courses taught you to be "tough".

It was all about Alpha dog and dominance and no other point of view would be taken into account.

I also took part in a course on search and rescue and carried out several interventions. At the same time, I started to look into agility as well.

I was willing to learn more and more, shadowing instructors and reading hundreds of books so after a while I started to follow the training of a few dogs independently without any particular problems.

In 1994 I held my first agility competition and in 1997 I decided to take over a dog training centre, starting a school with its own identity: ModenaDog.

In a short time we became a reference point for the area and, given our central position on the map of Italy, we hosted initiatives of great value.

Apart from agility, I paid particular attention to problematic dogs.

At that time, the 'Campbell test' was in vogue, a five-test evaluation system to which the puppy was subjected to in order to draw up a character profile.

Using it as a base, I created my own evaluation system by modifying a number of tests to complement an already innovative tool for the time.

Over the years different evaluations have been proposed, starting from analysing a complete motivational set designed to then be modified according to the dog's experiences and activities.

In 1998, with Emi still in great shape, I decided to bring a new friend into my life, Teo, a Labrador Retriever, who was always ready to work, but I had exaggerated his need for interaction, depriving him of the ability to remain calm.

I realised this when I decided to stop agility competitions and give Teo a pension worthy of his 'working' career. I learned at that moment that he was unable to relax and enjoy the sweet life.

The mistakes I had made were yet another confirmation that working on motivation had a great importance and a strong effect on the dog's character.

In December 2004 I left ModenaDog to create a new dog training centre, the DTC (Dog Training Centre Vignola) on a piece of land of over five thousand square metres.

The strength of the DTC was our team from the very beginning and the result was a place where puppy classes, educational courses, courses for problematic dogs, agility dogs, guided excursions, internships with top professionals and an endless series of initiatives filled the fourteen years of my management.

Over the years, the dog centre has also carried out projects with schools and sheltered facilities, and many different activities for our members. We also financed a humanitarian mission to Sierra Leone, contributing to the purchase of land for the construction of new schools.

In 2005 Smilla, a delightful Cavalier King Charles Spaniel, came into my life and contributed to my development for thirteen years.

In 2009, after a ten-year process, I became an ENCI Expert Agility Judge.

Then, in 2010, after Teo's passing, Thelma arrived, the chocolate Labrador that some of you may have seen in my videos.

At the same time I started home tuition, which had always fascinated me.

I have always been a fan of video editing, and with the arrival of smartphones everything became easier. Sending and receiving material via WhatsApp, I started to make short videos so I could give further support to the adopters and continuity in suggested activities.

Talking to Manu, my son, who was 11 at the time, we discussed people he followed on YouTube and the idea of setting up my own channel was born.

Learn to look at the world
through your dog's eyes

In November 2018, the decision was made to start the YouTube channel at the beginning of the new year. The filming technician was Manu, my son. He did not realise that he was going to become the 'supermegapowerdirector', as we jokingly call him. At the age of eleven, he was having fun playing web consultant, providing me with all his knowledge gained from following The Mates and other YouTube phenomenas.

My aim was to focus on giving value from a dog's point of view and understanding their emotions, which are far too often neglected. It is usually taken for granted that they should listen to us, follow us, respect us and be happy at the same time. "Learn to look at the world through your dog's eyes" because looking at reality from a dog's point of view would make everything so much easier. Focusing on this principle allows you to obtain the animal's best welfare and in this way, I am certain, great results and satisfaction will be achieved without too much of a struggle.

That's why my first film highlights this, taking a moment of Thelma's day as a typical situation.

So, in April 2019, I made a video entitled: *A dog in Modena.* The video was made by comparing what I was seeing with what the dog was seeing during our walk in the historic centre of Modena. What Thelma's eyes observed was in black and white.

You can watch it here:

Our videos

In the meantime, I started a collaboration with Nicola whose IT knowledge and experience could support and help me with my requests and ideas.

It was great to work with such a helpful and competent person, who I first met during agility competitions.

We went from 50 daily views in August 2019 to 5,000 in August 2020. And that was just the beginning.

Dogs are a very common topic on internet.

Many videos regarding dogs are very well made in terms of picture, sound and editing, but it's difficult to find simple and detailed solutions to problems.

Therefore, our main goal was to be simple, clear and to give people the chance to get some useful tips for everyday life.

Our target audience was the average person who doesn't have much time or has got financial restrictions which would not allow him/her to attend a dog centre or to call a behaviourist.

Of course you can watch the videos and still attend a dog centre.

Therefore, we have done our best to include tutorials as a support to the explanations, to create a kind of guide you can use in everyday life.

We have also included videos showing ordinary people's dogs, which represent real problems in real situations.

My aim is to give adopters useful tips making them as independent as possible when training their dogs.

This might be an unusual way of thinking, but I'm convinced this is the correct approach as it puts the adopters in the better position of actively building their exclusive relationship with their dogs.

This way it becomes possible to take the first steps of training in the most peaceful environment the dog knows, which is where he or she lives.

At times, my videos might have been repetitive with the concepts I wanted to be passed on, and this is precisely because I want people to have the impression that they are talking to me when they are watching a video, as if we were having a chat, rather than them being concentrated on a list of "to do things" from which to take notes.

Our tutorials follow a logical sequence that could suggest a working method for a complete training course and as the number of videos increased, we created themed *playlists*. We wanted the tutorials to be easy to find so, for example, people who are going to get a dog would find my suggestions on a playlist called *Waiting for your arrival.*

This seemed like a practical and effective way to liaise with me but the key point was that the topics could be handled independently by the user. A relationship would be created between the dog, the adopter and, why not, someone who would answer the adopter's questions through a video when needed.

Adopter? If you have a dog, feel like an adopter. I don't like to talk about ownership: you have adopted a dog, whether you have paid for them or been given them for free, you have in fact adopted them as they are not an object but a creature who is now part of your family.

Since I've been asked on several occasions how we create a tutorial, we thought it would be nice to make a video about the topic: *"How a tutorial is created"*.

Doga

During one of my competitions as an agility dog judge in 2019, I met Veronica, who was very passionate about her project to write a book on doga (yoga with a dog), combining her expertise with that of various professionals.

In her project *"My Doga"* my role would be linked to basic training, to allow the pair to approach this new discipline.

For you to have a better understanding of Veronica's project, I think the best thing to do is to leave it to her, so she can provide you with a better definition of her project.

The heart of 'My Doga'.

In order to be able to explain doga, it is necessary to summarise very quickly what yoga is.

The term yoga means 'union'. The root is yuj: "to bind together", "to hold tight". Many misunderstandings have arisen, since yoga - of millennial Indian origin - is neither a religion, nor a philosophical system, nor even a simple physical practice.

Yoga can be considered a 'particular' discipline, where the main purpose is to help us discover a path to unite our heart, body and mind as one, allowing us to develop a true awareness of who we are.

Specifically, doga is the combination of "yoga + dog" and consists of practising yoga with your dog. If for humans there are asanas, i.e. body posture, used as a tool for observing the potential and limits of our body, In dogs we can talk of dog-asana.

With regard to the fundamental breathing techniques of yoga, pranayama, and centring in the 'here and now', I would like to point out that in my project they involve not only humans, but the entire human-dog duo in order to achieve a deep connection as a couple, based on a shared physical, spiritual presence and pure love.

The discovery of yoga.

I started doing yoga several years ago and have never stopped, and I have always loved dogs. I practice agility and dog dance with my girls, but something different happens when I do yoga: I find Angy and Dreamy eager to play or receive cuddles on the mat. So the connection between dog walking and yoga was natural and immediate.

'My doga' was born from the union of my two greatest passions: the innate and deep love I have for animals, especially dogs and horses, and the strong physical and spiritual bond with yoga, which started my process of inner transformation, awareness and consciousness, that I hope will remain constantly and eternally in progress within me.

'My doga' is not just doga.

A kind of doga already exists in the world, but the substantial difference between the various existing forms of yoga with a dog and my doga is that in the project I am constructing, both beings that form the pair are considered individually, respecting the reciprocal differences of the species. In this way I would like to be able to bring intense wellbeing to both, transferring the necessary tools to regain this state independently, on the yoga mat and above all in the immense tapestry of life that is the world.

We must not forget that our partner is the dog and, as in any real and deep love relationship, we need to know our differences including our languages and the basics of our communication: from studying proxemics and the dog's main calming and stress signals, to understanding what the dog's motivations are.

In this sense, "My Doga" involves a concerted collaboration of professionals of the highest level, who are able to focus and make a specific contribution to the various aspects of the project. This is why we can consider it unique!

The main aim is to find a pleasant moment of renewed energy that rediscovers an ancestral friendship between humans and dogs, who learn to get to know each other and communicate in a union of bodies, hearts and minds.

The key to happiness.

What is needed is love, an awakening of conscience, a desire to learn or relearn to discover who we are in order to be happy, perhaps starting with a walk with our best friend. My doga puts together physical exercise and spirituality, which takes into account the differences between people and dogs and above all evokes the ancient pact of friendship and alliance that binds them.

All dogs can practice doga: small, medium and large dogs of any age. Obviously, differences must be taken into account in order to understand how to structure the lesson. The benefits are many, including therapeutic. In addition to breathing techniques, meditatio asanas for humans, dog-

21

asanas, as mentioned above, are also provided for dogs, as well as massages, cuddles and the use of essential oils. Everything is aimed to generate an energy of peace that can lead the couple to physical and spiritual well-being and deep relaxation.

Guna is a Sanskrit term which indicates the energy that surrounds all things. The term derives from the Indo-European 'gere', which means 'winding', indicating the single threads which create a rope. It gives the idea that nothing is possible without a real connection.

The tools.

To practice "My Doga" you need a specially designed mat for the pair, a second smaller mat, a cover for the dog, some targets and treats and a special harness with an extremely lightweight lead. "My doga" can be practised at home, outdoors or wherever you prefer.

I would like to end this presentation expressing my deep gratitude to all my precious collaborators, who are generously passing on their experience, help, advice and profound expertise which they have gained over the years: Marco Annovi, author of this book, who granted me space in his project, Lusy Imbergerova from "LuXaDer dogdance & tricks", Italian champion of freestyle and heelwork to music who is also my dog dance teacher; and Serena Fiorenzani, from Ovunqueyoga teacher training school, another one of my teachers who has practised yoga in both France and Italy.

I would like to remind you that this journey of mine is taking shape in a book, which I started writing a few months ago so as *to clarify and provide all the necessary elements to best tackle the journey within "My doga" YouTube channel.*

With this presentation Veronica Mancusi has provided all the necessary information about her project and I personally feel honoured to be part of it.

A parallel point of view

Radja: I owe a lot to her.

A female border collie of rare beauty.

I took her from a kennel in Ravenna in August 2013, where she was born on 3rd June.

It was love at first sight: I was looking for a dynamic dog that would fit into my lifestyle and border collies are perfect in that respect. But Radja ended up doing much more for me!

Among other things, it was thanks to her that I was able to get to know this breed, but above all I was able to study it and over time admire it more and more for the way they interact and work, which is truly unique.

I was so fascinated by it that the family immediately expanded: my wife got another border collie, a male called Alvin, and then along came the third one, Winny, who is Radja's daughter.

When Radja arrived, I didn't understand anything about dogs. Radja had a very pronounced kinesthetic motivation that I was absolutely unable to manage. I must admit that I had started doing agility without any expertise.

But all of this led me to something great: meeting Marco and solving my problems with Radja.

Without Radja, therefore, probably this book wouldn't exist either.

By combining our respective skills, mine in graphic design and computer science and his in video editing and cynophilia, Marco and I created the AmDogTraining YouTube channel.

Nicola Atzori

I met Nicola a few years ago during an agility competition: I was the judge and he was one of the competitors with his Border Collie. Thanks to his advanced computer skills – he is a computer technician – he is responsible for the graphic aspects and the direction of all the online courses.

He is the co-founder of AmDog Training.

Part two

Identify yourself with the solution, not with the problem
(T.Y.S. Lama Gangchen)

Is the dog too excitable? Here's what to do

Four practical exercises to try and solve the problems.

I published a tutorial on my YouTube channel suggesting four exercises to do with an overexcited dog to help him regain his composure.

When it comes to exuberant, overexcited dogs, the causes can be many and sometimes of unknown origin.

It is wrong to stimulate their excitement.

In these cases most adopters would start exercise activities with the illusion of making the dog calmer but in doing so they are merely "training" the predisposition that has been manifested. This can be explained by analysing the motivations that are stimulated through common games, for example chasing the ball or tug-of-war. We often overlook the fact that these sort of activities act on the predatory, possessive and kinesthetic motivations which, translated into simple words, will respectively stimulate the dog to chase anything that moves, make him feel like the owner of an object and increase his desire to run. All of this is self-perpetuating and the dog will progressively increase these behaviours. One question I often ask people is "*How do puppies play with each other?*" and I already know the answer:

"They jump on each other and bite". Consequently, we have to create different dynamics, otherwise they will continue to interact in the same way. We need to offer activities that promote calm, self-control and attention. Here are four simple exercises to start with, preferably following the sequence suggested below and also watching the video in the link.

1) THE ZEN DOGGY

This aims to encourage the dog to seek our gaze, in order to gain permission and approval and to improve his/her attention towards us.

Keep a treat in one hand, let the dog sniff it in order to create an expectation and place the hand on the side of your body about 20 cm away from the animal's head. Initially your dog will come up with the repertoire they usually use for attention: jumping on us, nibbling on our hands, barking and since none of these rituals will lead to a result, at a certain point they will look at us. Right at that time they will get the treat. This will be repeated at different times in front of doors, gates, when getting out of the car etc thus creating a sort of request for permission, which passes through a look in our eyes.

2) FOOD

The aim is to teach the dog to sit and wait for permission to eat. Again we will work on self-control and attention, training the dog to focus on us.

Watching the adopters I realised that the permission to eat is, in most cases, automatically given by putting the bowl on the floor. Often the dog would start jumping during the preparation phase. What we should do instead is, as soon as we have the bowl in our hands, we remain in front of the dog without saying a word or making any requests. The dog, after several attempts that do not lead to any result, will finally try to sit, obtaining as a reward the arrival of the bowl. It may be that the dog, whenever the bowl touches the ground, will automatically approach it to eat, but at that point, without speaking, raise the bowl again. The message that must be understood by the dog is that if he approaches the food without our permission, the bowl will be raised. We will then start to use a hand to give permission to eat.

3) THE RECALL

This third exercise aims to control moments of absolute freedom. Usually the recall represents a negative situation as it is perceived as "end of freedom". This is because we normally call the dog back every time we have to put the leash back on. The recall must become a positive experience, as if the dog thinks: "How nice, you called me, I'll come and get a reward and then I'll go back to do what I was doing".

How does recall work with dogs? They get down on their front limbs, turn around 180 degrees and walk away, inviting the other dogs to chase them. We must do the same, turn our heads to the opposite side and move away, calling the dog back with a simple verbal request: "Come here!". When the dog comes to us, all we need to do is to reward them and let them go back to what they were doing. This sequence must be repeated ten times over a period of ten minutes. Nine times we will let the dog free to go back to what they were doing and the tenth time we will put the leash on. All of this should be done in an enclosed area or in a protected environment. Otherwise we should use a long training lead for safety and security.

4) THE TWO-BALL GAME

Usually, an excited dog uses the ball to engage us in activities in which they are the winner: the possession of the ball is their trophy. We need to change their perception with the following exercise:

Throw the ball, the dog will go for it. If you used to chase them or repeatedly ask them to bring the ball back to you, this time you will turn your back and go to the opposite side playing with a second ball in your hands. You will see that the dog will undoubtedly come to you, with or without the ball in their mouth. At that point you will give them the second ball, retrieving the first and repeating the same procedure. Bear in mind that it will not be necessary to throw the ball metres away, but it will be more useful to wait for the dog to be near us and then give it to them as soon as they sit down. After ten minutes we will end the playful moment with a clear gesture that will mean "end of the game". At a later stage we will repeat the same structured method of giving food with the difference that this time instead of food we will have a ball.

Happy Birthday, Kong!

I published two tutorials on my YouTube channel about the Kong.: the first video, *Playing with the Kong*, I presented it in all its effectiveness, describing how to use it and all its potential when used correctly. In the second video, *Kong, instructions for use!* I listed all the responses the dog might give as a result of wrong approaches, providing the necessary corrections for each situation. The Kong was created in 1970 by Joe Markham, whose dog Fritz was a destructive chewer. One day Mr.Markham gave the dog a piece of a rubber suspension off a Volkswagen van. The hard-to-control snowman shape of the rubber was perfect for such a resilient dog and it immediately became his favourite toy. Impressed by his discovery, Markham began the production of what has since become one of the best-selling items in the dog toy market.

The Kong is made of rubber in a honeycomb shape with a cavity inside so that it can be filled with food. It is extremely safe even if subjected to continuous chewing and can become an excellent training instrument. On the website www.kongcompany.com, which is simple and intuitive to use, you will find everything you need to know about it: which one to choose depending on the size and needs of your dog, what you can fill it with depending on your dog's abilities, etc. And why does the dog like it so much?

Chewing and using the mouth are natural activities for dogs.

Using the Kong you give your dog a way to satisfy one of their needs in a healthy way for both of you (so you won't have your house destroyed) following certain rules.

Using the Kong, the dog's goal is to reach the treats inside. But it is not so easy for him to achieve this, as the toy is resistant to biting and may bounce around erratically.

The animal has to develop his own skills to get the treats. The activity combines the use of the paws and mouth in a coordinated manner, thus promoting proprioception and mental activity.

We ask the dog to sit down, start preparing the Kong by filling it with the right food, place it in front of him or hide it, and when we are ready we give the dog permission to start searching for the Kong and the treasure inside it.

Clearly there will be different levels of difficulties related to the content put inside: small dog biscuits will come out much more easily than bigger ones or soft treats.

Using the Kong correctly we will provide the dog with an activity while staying at home, preventing boredom and related destructive behaviour; promote the dog's self-control and concentration, reduce separation anxiety; promote a state of relaxation and tranquillity resulting from masticatory activity.

In order to achieve all these beneficial effects, there are certain rules to follow.

Initially you need to make it easy for the dog to get the treats and increase the difficulties just very gradually. Working step by step if it becomes too difficult for the dog to get the treats, you can go back to an easier level, always making sure that your dog can get pleasure and gratification from the activity .

It is you who will provide your four-legged companion with the skills to cope with increasing difficulties.

Remember that a real activity has to be set up with clear signals defining the beginning, the duration and the end.

Specifically, you will need to know how to teach the 'sit' or 'down' position, and the 'stay' and 'leave' command, because the actual exercise will also have a preparation phase.

First, you will ask the dog to sit or lie down and place the Kong in front of them, in an upright position at a distance of 50 cm. Then you will place a tasty treat at 10 cm in front or to the side of the Kong. When ready you will give the "go" signal with your hand.

In this first stage, the Kong will be close to the treat, but not in contact: doing so you will let the dog get used to the new object, and concentrate their focus on the reward.

In the following stages you will place the treat closer and closer to the toy, until you finally place it under the Kong.

The dog, in order to get the treat, will naturally use the snout to move the toy to reach the treat..

You will then gradually raise the difficulties. Each time the dog gets the treat, you will call them to your side or in front of you and start again challenging them with a new difficulty.

Possible difficulties:

Problem: The dog shows no interest in the Kong.

Solution: Try a more appetising, special reward and be sure to get the dog's attention on the treat to be obtained.

Problem: The dog does not stay still during the preparation.

Solution: Does the dog correctly "sit" or "lie down" and remain still until we give permission to move? Work on these exercises separately, starting with simple situations such as feeding.

Problem: The dog fails to bite the toy and consequently stops at some point and gives up.

Solution: You might have chosen a type of Kong which could be too hard or of the wrong size for your dog. On the official Kong website you can find guidance to making the correct choice according to the characteristics of your animal. The hardness of the object is differentiated by its colour. The size clearly varies according to the size of the mouth.

Problem: The dog goes straight to the Kong and bites it and/or carries it around.

Solution: Work on the palatability of the reward and

discourage the dog's interest in the toy as they probably perceive it as a ball. When you ask the dog to sit or lie down, try to teach them first to go, with your permission, for the treat initially without using the Kong.

Problem: The dog, after getting the treats, continues to bite the Kong and does not leave it.

Solution: Does your dog know "leave"? If not, work on it taking a step back and abandoning the Kong for the moment, otherwise the dog will learn not to "leave" when you ask them in everyday life.

Problem: The dog does not pay attention and gets distracted.

Solution: Always choose quiet, familiar *locations* where your dog will be able to pay attention to you. Also keep working sessions very short and always stop whilst the dog still feels rewarded and is still interested in following the exercises you propose.

Things that you absolutely need to avoid:

Using the Kong as a ball, for the simple reason that its correct use would help the dog to feel calmer, while using it as a ball would stimulate their predatory motivation and possible competition.

Continuing the exercises until the dog is no longer interested.

Skipping initial steps that you consider unimportant. It would be like starting to make a cake without checking that you have all the necessary ingredients first: you might find yourself having to stop halfway through to go to the supermarket. Skipping the steps would make the training unpleasant for you too.

Overly difficult situations: your dog needs to develop their skills gradually to keep their attention and be willing to cooperate and play with you.

To conclude, the dog is keen to learn whatever we suggest in a systematic manner. Just think of all the times you have noticed that your dog was able to understand what you were about to do just by observing you. The problem is that often we don't make a good use of the dog's natural ability when we manage their learning process.

For example we can be unclear and assume that the dog would very quickly understand what we are asking him in many different ways. In the first video I published I said that we need to *Learn to see the world through your dog's eyes* and I am still convinced it is the key to a good mutual understanding between you and your dog.

The perfect eight-point walk

If we have a dog, then going for a daily walk is a truly relaxing and regenerating moment. It becomes a habit and a moment of socialisation, a fixed appointment to switch off. However, adopters often have bad habits, poor organisation, distractions, lack of time, etc., so the supposedly pleasant walk turns into something hasty and the poor dog becomes overwhelmed by our unpredictable and chaotic life, without gaining any benefit. On my YouTube channel "AmDogTraining" there is a specific playlist called *The Walk* where I have collected five videos that can help you with details to improve one of the main problems that you face every day when you have a dog.

Why is it so difficult to walk in peace?

The dog was not born to be on a leash and, moreover, we often make our requests in a way that is not appropriate. Choke collars, energetic tugging on the leash and many other "solutions" that initially seem to solve the problem, in fact are obvious errors in the dog's perspective. If we take the dog to places that present a lot of distractions for them and we ask them to walk by our side when they are still not familiar with this exercise, we will not get a relaxed walk. In a video I have explained five basic points on how to correctly set up a walk with our dog. I'll also add another three tips to help you improve your walks with your dog. It is always important to try to look at the different situations through your dog's eyes and focus on helping them with the learning process.

1) ONE AND A HALF METRE LEASH

Let's start with the tool we are going to use. I recommend using a soft, lightweight lead, no more than one and a half metres long. Many people ask me: "Why not use an extendable lead?". Because an extendable lead will probably always be in traction. This means that the dog will become used to being pulled continuously and in any case, will learn to pull to try to go where they want, remember that the dog will learn to walk on a lead without pulling if you don't use the lead to prevent them from pulling. This means that in practice, if you want your dog to stay close to you without pulling, you will have to work hard to find "interesting reasons " to get them to follow you without the lead preventing them from walking away.

2) COLLAR OR HARNESS?

Starting from the fact that I want the dog to choose to remain at my side I recommend the harness as it doesn't act on the neck which is a particularly important relational area.

3) TO THE RIGHT OR LEFT?

Strictly left-handed training was due to the fact that the first manuals referred to "military" dogs and then, over the years, left-handed conduct continued.

In my opinion either side is ok as long as it is always the same so that position will over time become a "comfort zone" to receive gratification and the starting point for exercises, and activities. As this is a comfortable and pleasant position, you should make sure that you always use a soft lead whenever you have your dog by your side. The lead will be held with the right hand if we keep the dog on the right, with the left hand if we hold them on the left. The opposite hand will be the one that gives instructions and becomes a reference point for the dog.

4) AN ACTIVITY TO DO TOGETHER

The walk is a valuable moment for the dog to share with us interacting and exchanging information. How can this happen if the dog is concentrating on his own business and we are on the phone or on the internet? Starting with just a few metres, try to walk that distance paying attention to your dog and looking for their interest in you. Of course, you can use anything that makes you look interesting - a ball, a nice treat, anything that will draw the dog's gaze to you will work.

5) AN IDEAL PLACE TO START

As your goal is to get your dog's attention, it will be easier when disturbances and distractions are reduced to a minimum, that is at home. I therefore suggest that you start "leading" your dog by structuring a real "domestic" walk. In that context it will be much easier for your dog to follow you and you'll become familiar with the lead. Should you decide to start in a quiet but unfamiliar environment, then allow the dog time to inspect it and wait until they feel calm and able to connect with you. When you start to include difficulties and disturbing elements always do this very gradually and continue to expose your dog to positive experiences.

6) HOW TO ORGANISE THE FIRST OUTDOOR WALKS

Rather than walking miles, just do a few metres together. Rather than walking on a straight path, it would also be much easier for the dog to follow short sequences with circular trajectories and changes of direction. Keep time very short: 2, 3 or 5 minutes only and always end when your dog is still focused on you. Enrich the short walk with playful moments and some simple exercises that will help your dog to stay focused on you. The attention span will only lengthen naturally if you manage to work well and do not cause your dog to perceive what you do together as a source of stress and fatigue.

7) MEETING OTHER DOGS

Socialising and interacting with other dogs is a fundamental moment that improves your dog's sociality but, as always in your relationship with your dog, you need to be able to give clear rules. Sociality is the dog's ability to experience social relationships with people and other animals in a positive manner. However, we often see dogs who want to interact with every dog they meet. There will be times when we favour the interaction, while in other circumstances we won't and instead we'll propose interesting alternatives in order to make the dog feel less interested in the new encounter. Regarding the moments of interaction between dogs, they must take place in neutral areas and especially with dogs off the lead, as it would often reduce communication and increase tensions between the animals, creating dynamics which sometimes could be dangerous. Consequently, whenever possible, go for walks within fenced areas and then leave the dogs free to interact.

8) WHAT IF OUR DOG PULLS ON THE LEAD?

Whether it is a dog who is new to walking or a chronic "lead puller", we should not prevent them from pulling, but we should encourage them to keep close to us. In the case of a puppy or a dog who is new to walking this will be much easier. We will plan the walks working on small activities aimed to keep the dog's attention on us. If, on the other hand, we have a dog who had negative experiences in this respect, we will need to invest more time in creating alternatives that they will find more interesting than repeating what they had previously learned. We must always remember that the dog will only repeat behaviours that lead them to achieve a goal and, consequently, we need to change their goal. You need to propose alternatives and new ways of interacting and stop giving value to dynamics that have been supported up until now. You need to make sure that every time the lead is not in traction you give value to this event.

CONCLUSION:

I will close by reiterating what I said at the beginning: dogs are not born to be on a lead, but we can make the walk a pleasant event for them by relieving the lead itself of the burden and responsibility of preventing the dog from pulling. This is the way to teach our best friend to stay by our side in a pleasant way.

Does the dog bite? Train him/her from puppyhood

One of the most common problems for adopters is that the dog is mouthy. But have you ever wondered where this behaviour originates? Before you get into situations that may be difficult to manage in adult dogs, is there anything you can do to address this in a puppy? How can you correct this annoying 'way of communicating' that your dog uses? To answer these questions I have published two videos on the AmDogTraining channel, where I explain how to intervene immediately and how to plan activities that discourage the use of the mouth. As is my habit, instead of focusing on the final problem, I like to search for the causes of it. When people ask me for a quick solution to the problem, I usually ask: "How do dogs interact with each other?". And the answer I receive is: "Jumping on each other and biting". The dog would take this for granted if no one suggests alternative ways of interacting and it would be natural for them to repeat a behaviour that they have learned from the first days of their life.

THE USE OF THE MOUTH

A puppy's way of playing involves the use of the mouth. When we take the dog home and start tug-of-war and ball games or even play wrestling using our hands we reinforce this behaviour and give the dog confirmation that this is the right way to interact, so we are creating the basis of what can become a serious problem in adulthood.

PUPPIES AND EARLY SEPARATION FROM THE MOTHER

There can be a number of situations that encourage the biting behaviour from early life.

One of the main causes is premature separation from the mother. The law is clear: it is forbidden to take puppies away from their mothers before they are 60 days old, a time limit indicated by vets as the optimal time for the puppy's correct socio-cognitive development in intra- and interspecific relations.

BITE INHIBITION

Never hurry to separate the puppy from their mother. An early separation, in fact, could have serious repercussions on the psycho-physical health of the animal. It is also important to clarify what is simplistically defined as "bite inhibition". There are lots of videos on the web recommending "bite inhibition" in puppies through a series of activities, but I don't fully agree. I have rarely heard of the importance to the animal of being able to use its mouth. In fact, the dog originally used its mouth as a tool for hunting, attacking, defending and grasping. Regarding the mouth being used as a weapon, it would be appropriate to invest time in creating interactions aiming to moderate its use and avoiding the situations where the dog feels they have to show a defensive behaviour and, consequently, use the mouth as a "weapon". From a certain perspective we ask our dogs not to behave according to their nature and that is why, rather than 'inhibiting' the bite it seems to me more appropriate to 'regulate' it. Chewing can also be a pleasant activity for the dog, providing relaxation if disciplined in well-defined activities. So, biting and chewing can be used to our advantage when they become an additional rewarding and gratifying activity for our companions.

WHY DOES THE PUPPY BITE?

Puppies, just like infants, begin to explore the world through their mouths. They lick, bite, nibble and chew on countless things in order to learn about the world. Even earlier, when teeth are growing, biting is a way to relieve the discomfort. The first social interactions involve the use of the mouth as well. In moments of boredom chewing an object can become a useful activity, the same as it can be relaxing to relieve anxiety or when the dog becomes very excited. That is why in certain situations destructive activities are more likely to occur.

Here is a list of the main causes which can tempt a young dog to annoyingly bite at everything:

- Early detachment from the mother.

- Large litter.

- Inexperienced mother (young or first litter).

- Mother taken away from her puppies (unfortunately there are breeders who still do this) therefore they will be deprived of their mother's contact.

- Breeds which have been selected for activities involving intensive use of the mouth (e.g. Shepherd Dogs, Terriers etc.).

- Toys or objects like cloths, rags or similar that encourage predatory motivation and the use of the mouth.

- Games played at home (tug-of-war, ball, etc).

HOW TO INTERVENE?

A detailed assessment and advice from an expert is the best way forward to avoid further complications that would affect the pleasure of sharing our life with a dog.

Motivation is the impulse that naturally leads a dog to act in certain ways rather than others. Biting involves predatory and kinesthetic motivations. If we encourage activities that feed these   motivations, the dog will continue to show biting behaviour. If we want to reduce biting we need to introduce collaborative, communicative and search motivations, trying to help the dog to be calm and self-controlled. On AmDogTraining channel you can find a video about how to reduce or encourage a motivation.

EIGHT ACTIONS TO TAKE

1) FREEZE, NO RESPONSE - As much as possible, freeze and ignore the behaviour you want to reduce. For example, if the puppy bites one of your hands, remain as still as possible. Any yelp or action would still be a response and dogs only propose and repeat actions that lead to a response.

2) IGNORE - If possible, ignore and leave the room or place. This way the dog will try to follow you and stop biting.

3) PROPOSE SOMETHING ELSE - Avoid pulling and triggering competition and propose an alternative like a treat, always being careful not to let the dog think that biting will get them a treat.

4) DIRECT THE DOG'S ATTENTION TOWARDS SOMETHING DIFFERENT - Throw a few treats on the ground and start a scent search.

5) DISCIPLINE ACTIVITIES - any activity has to be well defined with a clear beginning and a clear end. This includes intense exercise, as at the end of any activity our goal is to make the dog calm.

6) CONTEXTUALISING - when the dog bites they are giving us the information that biting is something interesting to them. We can use this information, contextualising it and moving the dog's attention onto toys such as the Kong or other objects that are suitable to be chewed on.

7) CONFIRMING WANTED BEHAVIOURS - Don't try to eliminate the behaviours you want to control (and don't punish your dog), but encourage the ones you want. This means that you need to work on alternatives when your dog behaves in a way you don't want, and on confirmations when the dog shows behaviours that you do want.

8) SOCIALISATION WITH OTHER DOGS - Encourage socialisation but select your dog's "friends" as calmer ones may help to compensate your dog's characteristics. However, this may be difficult to achieve if you do not have the necessary skills.

DISCOURAGING BITING: FOUR ACTIVITIES TO REGULATE
THE USE OF THE MOUTH

- Kong or problem solving (mental activation games) and games where the use of the mouth is involved, but in a controlled way. The important thing is to always create a structure with a beginning and an end, and to discipline everything. Prohibiting your dog from biting will only increase their desire to do so. Instead, if you contextualise their biting, you will manage to moderate a natural predisposition;

- Teaching the dog to "leave": if we ask the dog to leave a toy just when we decide to stop playing they will associate "leave" with something negative. Instead of doing this, we need to use "leave" as a part of of our activities together. A difference must be made between something that can be bitten but must be left when requested and something that cannot be bitten. This will improve the dog's self-control and lower their excitement;

- Searching activities which involve a reward that the dog can chew which will lead to satisfaction and relaxation.

- Use of the blanket to encourage relaxation; you can also massage and brush your dog: if this gets done methodically and carefully, it can create a cosy moment. These activities will promote interactions where the dog keeps calm and has self-control.

Regarding self-control, there are specialists who associate it with the dog's ability to sit or lie down for a long time if requested, which is something I disapprove of.

Does your dog jump on you?

This is certainly one of the most common problems, but also a dog's natural behaviour, so it is normal if they jump on us looking for a cuddle or "greeting" visitors by jumping up.

WE NEVER ASSESS THE DOG'S MOTIVATION.

We usually focus on the problem that is bothering us without considering the real motivation that leads the dog to behave in a certain way. Dogs jump on each other in search of attention, to make requests and sometimes to clarify the hierarchy within the group. We often stimulate and confirm these habits, especially when it comes to small dogs.

NO CONFLICT, BUT INTERACTION.

At the beginning of my career in dog training, to overcome this problem, I had been advised by several dog trainers to use my knee to make the dog feel something unpleasant and negative. All this was in line with the methods used at that time. Again, we were focusing on stopping unwanted dog's behaviours. My way of interacting with the dog changed radically when I realised that it is more important to propose what we want, working on permissions and finding a way forward together in a positive way. All of this must be based on mutual trust, whilst in the past, dog training was based on conflict.

On the AmDogTraining YouTube channel you can find two videos about how to train your dog not to jump on you. The first one, with text and explanations, gives you suggestions on how to deal with the topic and it is easy to understand. The second video belongs to the didactic series and has been produced without any text or commentary, but with images only. It is only visual, but complete. The videos were produced during a consultation with an adopter who was seeking help regarding this dog's behaviour. So you can see how to act in everyday life regarding this topic.

TEN TIPS TO DISCOURAGE THIS ANNOYING BEHAVIOUR
On the AmDogTraining YouTube channel you can find detailed tutorials.

1) Ignore the dog whenever they jump on you and offer alternatives that will make them keep their paws down. Even a simple "no", "stop it!", a look or anything else you can think of to discourage this behaviour will instead give the dog a response and will have the opposite effect.

2) Use exercises such as giving the food in the correct way, asking the dog to wait for your permission to get their meal.

3) Use activities like "Doggy zen" to encourage your dog to focus on you.

4) Whilst playing with toys that get thrown, prefer the "sit" or "down" position as a starting point and make sure the dog does not have to jump to get the toy.

5) When you "recall" your dog, get on your knees and reward them with a treat at ground level.

6) Propose exercises such as 'high-five', 'give paw' to promote a conscious use of the paws.

7) If there are small children in the family always pay attention to managing the interaction between the dog and the child carefully to avoid triggering dangerous situations: a small child is usually at eye level with the dog and the line between a playful moment and a confrontational moment is very thin.

8) Work on self-control with activities that lower your dog's excitement and, as a result, you will have a calmer animal in every situation. Heightened *excitement* leads to a loss of self-control, often causing the dog to be restless and to engage in kinesthetically motivated activities. To work on self-control

and calmness means practising activities that will teach the dog to wait, to use the sense of smell and to "think", promoting collaborative and communicative motivations.

9) During walks reward your dog when they are walking alongside you and not only when sitting.

10) If you have a small dog, it might be more complicated, but you have to put yourself on the same level as them in every way.

It will also be very important to give friends and people who interact with the dog instructions on how to behave with the dog in order to maintain consistency. No matter the location and the people interacting with the dog, the rules should always be the same.

Management

What are the right considerations to make when we decide to bring a dog into our lives in order to minimise any unpleasant surprises that might compromise our cohabitation?.

Years ago dog training was based on the concept that dogs originate from wolves and, consequently you had to be the pack leader or you wouldn't get respect, and you had to work using a leash.

Let's now consider the differences between a pack in the woods and the dogs in our homes, between life in the mountains and days spent in a flat sleeping on a bed.

HIERARCHIES AND HERDS

Let's take a step back. "So the pack is a family structure based on the pair and the offspring of one or more years, on average 7/8 elements, rarely 15/20". With this sentence the veterinary behaviourist Barbara Gallicchio, in her book *Lupi travestiti. Le origini biologiche del cane domestico* (Edizioni Cinque), describes a pack. The individuals live, hunt and move together, protecting their territory and raising their pups. In order for this to work, there are clear rules that organise life on a daily basis, preventing internal conflicts and resolving issues in a positive way for the survival of all. According to the herd hierarchy, each individual has a clearly defined place and tasks. There are roles and affiliations: a task of a given individual and feedback from those who represent the reference point. Despite the fact that wolves and dogs have been on different evolutionary paths for thousands of years, our dogs perceive the family in which they live as a pack. And as just described, there must also be clear roles and affiliations within our pack-family.

ALPHA PAIR AND TOP DOG

At the top of the wolf hierarchy is the 'alpha pair', i.e. the male and female who are responsible for protecting all the other members and coordinating the group's activities. The alpha pair are the ones which the others members defer to, following their directives, and it is also the pair that reproduces. The alpha male and female are the leaders of the herd and are trusted by all members as they are recognised for their intelligence, maturity, balance, competence and consistency. Being pack leader is a role of great effort and complexity. I would like to clarify what the usual dynamics in a pack are, which in certain respects are also recognised by our dog, to make you reflect on the difficulties that can be encountered in a management of this type. I repeat, life within a pack is different from what we propose to a family dog. In the latter case, in fact, our dog has difficulty in recognising a reference guide if we do not focus on small details of great value. We must pay attention to the roles and dynamics in our home from the moment we include a dog in our "pack". These considerations are even more important if we are going to have more than one dog, so in this case it will be necessary to organise a proper introduction.

WE ARE THEIR GUIDE

We'll need to manage the role of pack leader, becoming a guide and a reference for our dogs. We must be aware however, that conflicts and controversies will be normal, and that life in the pack is faced day by day as a group, while this is not always possible in our reality. Therefore it will be important to be accredited rather than dominant thus reducing the possibility of unpleasant misunderstandings.

HOW TO GET ACCREDITED IN THE FAMILY PACK

Manage food sources correctly - Food is a main bond: on several occasions during the day we can handle the feeding ritual through rules and clear signals.

Manage your dog's toys - In order to have "interesting topics" during our interactions with the dog, it is advisable to use toys they are particularly interested in and we should keep them and offer them at our discretion.

Encourage collaboration - Boost collaborative motivation by proposing activities where communication between the pair is paramount, clear and effective.

Suggest activities that strengthen the relationship - Always remember that your dog needs to be active, so play and engage their mind. You have two options: submit to the activities your dog chooses or be proactive and make them feel interested in what you propose. Of course I suggest the latter.

Think "together" and develop mutual trust - A healthy and balanced relationship must be built on trust. Whenever you propose negative situations or use ploys to achieve something that restricts the dog in their activities, you get immediate results that will create false associations over time and cause you to lose credibility. The typical example is the "recall", when the dog does not respond to your "Come here!". The dog's non-response is due to the association of your recall to a limitation of their freedom because when they come to you, they will be put on a lead sometimes interrupting activities that are interesting to him.

What if you have more dogs in the family?

Things become more complicated when there are several dogs in a family. While a natural pack is generally formed by the parents and their offspring, the group in a household is most often the result of decisions made by humans, often based on illogical criteria. We must always remember that being a pack leader and managing a group is an onerous and responsible role. This requires commitment and dedication: being a good pack leader means having fewer concerns and less stress for yourself and for the dogs.

TEN TIPS TO BECOME A TRUSTABLE PACK LEADER

1) Avoid confrontation and propose alternatives
We have to build a relationship, so it will be more important to indicate what we want with a positive feedback rather than concentrating on what we want to eliminate. Clashes only lead to conflict and tension. Alternatives and indications must become our goal.

2) Look after your dog's well-being
Pay attention to calming and stress signals during any activity. Encourage calmness, self-control and activities that bring your dog to tranquillity. Encourage interaction and communication.

3) Do not make rituals when entering or leaving the house
Avoid amplifying the moments when you leave your dog alone. When you return, take your time and only after several minutes you will be ready for greetings and attention. As far

as entry and exit are concerned, we can also talk about threshold management, i.e. training your dog to go through gates, main doors and get out of cars only when you give your consent. In the AmDogTraining YouTube channel you can find tutorial where I explain that a dog who runs out of gates and gets out of the car without waiting for a sign from us is interpreting the open gate or car door as a signal authorising them to go. My training method has the goal of getting the pet used to looking for our gaze to get feedback.

4) Ignore the activities proposed by the dog, but propose them at a time of your own choice.

If the dog brings you a ball and invites you to play, you should not do it but wait and then propose it later at your discretion. Dogs are very good trainers and train us to respond to their requests: playing with a ball, getting cuddles, etc. Dogs will always propose again any activities that get some form of response . This also includes any *"no"*, *"stop"* , screaming or any other feedback.

Considering the dog's suggestions, you can anticipate their preferences, but you always need to manage the start, progress and end of the activities.

5) Offer interactive walks

It is a good idea to construct the walk as a relaxing moment to be enjoyed together. Give priority to quiet environments.

6) Remember the importance of the feeding ritual
As already described, there are a number of clear messages behind the feeding ritual that make it valuable.

7) Relocate sleeping and kennel areas
Find an area where your pet can sleep in peace and that is not in privileged and controlling positions. Avoid beds, sofas or places that allow him/her to check all the movements of family members. It is the leaders who are responsible for defending the territory and taking care of the other members of the pack, controlling and supervising from privileged positions.

8) Maintain exclusive positions
It will be important for you to have an armchair, a sofa, a room or at least some exclusive place that makes it clear that you have a privileged role in relation to the dog.

9) Manage playtime and toys in a controlled way
Propose structured activities with a beginning, a middle and an end. Prioritise activities that favour searching, retrieving and communicative motivations. The toys should only be used during the activities.

10) Manage moments of social interaction

Any intra- or interspecific interaction should be evaluated and monitored. When you take your pet to the dog area let them interact only with dogs that show positive attitudes by selecting playmates. Avoid situations that allow the dog to become the "king" of the area and those that would put them in a stressful position having to face particularly "violent" attitudes and do not justify this with "they must understand how life works".

A GOOD LEADER DOES NOT USE THEIR STRENGTH

A good leader finds approval without the need to use their strength or coercive methods. If we are good at proposing this model as well, we will succeed in having a healthy and balanced relationship with the dog. A good leader manages to reach their audience through communication. Suggesting a way to do so is quite difficult considering it is such a vast subject and given the variables involved in each individual case. Differences in breeds, age of the dog, living environment, family unit, habits and different situations represent a number of combinations that should be analysed in detail. If you are new to dog training or are dealing with particularly demanding breeds, do not hesitate to contact a professional dog trainer or visit a dog centre: clarifying the situation from the very beginning is the basis for a peaceful future. Knowing how to communicate with your dog, understanding how to handle them, understanding their needs and how to interact correctly will allow you to seem more reliable and coherent. We must always remember that it is not our strength that makes us good leaders but our knowledge of the dog's ethology.

In a flat or in a garden?
Pros, cons and cautions

How many times have we heard "I won't get a dog because I don't have a garden" or "a dog shouldn't live in a flat"? But are we really sure that dogs want a garden?

In many years of home consultations I have come across dogs living in large gardens and others living in one-bedroom flats without even a balcony. What makes a dog happy? What does the dog really need in terms of its living environment?

Let's start as usual by looking at things from the animal's point of view.

All the individuals belonging to a natural pack all live together 24/7. Consequently, the first thing to understand is that in a pack it is necessary to live and share as many moments as possible together.

But let's look at the possibilities in practice.

APARTMENT

Pros:

-The dog will constantly experience our presence and will be able to observe us in detail.

-By paying attention to small management rules, there will be more chances of having a calm dog that is used to people and social interactions.

-It will be easier to have a balanced relationship.

-As well as the time spent together at home, walks will also be of considerable importance.

Cons:

-Because the dog is looking at us constantly, it will be necessary to be in 'perfect dog trainer ' mode at all times.

-"It's Saturday", "it's Sunday", "it's raining", "I'm tired" and "I don't feel in the mood today" are not acceptable justifications.

-"Wee-wee" and "poo-poo" will be situations to live with from the first days after arrival.

-When the dog is left alone there is a risk they might cause some damage.

Things we need to remember

-A gradual preparation will be needed before the dog can be left at home alone

-Keep exclusive spaces and situations for yourself.

GARDEN

Pros:

-No problems with uncontrolled dog faeces.

-The chances of damage to the interior of the house will be reduced, if not eliminated.

Cons:

-Little social experience.

-Possible management difficulties, due to the role of "guardian" conferred on the dog.

-Relying on a hypothetical well-being in outdoor life, we relegate the dog to social isolation, creating a series of problems that play against socialisation.

-Difficulties in relaxing, as there are many activities the dog can do

Things we need to remember:

-The dog is a social animal and needs to share experiences with us.

Avoid leaving the dog in the garden, managing their own time.

-Invest time in walks and activities to interact with the dog.

-Use the garden as a base to start activities.

-Please note that no matter how big the garden is, the dog will always use the same spaces, and these will usually be close to doors or gates. In any case, these areas will need to be protected.

-Place the dog's bed or kennel away from the access to the garden to avoid that the dog feels entitled to have control of the gate or door and can have a more relaxed rest.

OPTIMAL SITUATION

If we have to look for the optimum solution, it is clear that the best condition is to live in a house with a small garden.

I would like to point out, however, that neither of these

situations excludes the possibility of having a dog, providing that the necessary care is taken.

Consideration must be given to the dog's age, breed and individual experiences. A puppy will find it more difficult than an adult dog to be alone without causing damage. Certain breeds are more predisposed to live outdoors than others and are less affected by being alone. It is therefore difficult to establish rules that apply to everyone. Talking about breeds, try to think that a dog whose breed has been selected precisely "to keep you company", will suffer more from your absence compared to, for instance, a shepherd dog.

Considering that most people work from Monday to Friday, the time spent with the dog is usually concentrated on the weekend. A number of considerations need to be made here. Separation is one of the main causes of stress in dogs, no matter whether in a garden or in a flat. A stressful situation of a few hours requires a recovery time of two to six days; so if the dog is in distress all week, on Saturdays and Sundays it will be difficult to keep them calm and this will have a negative impact on the dog's and our own well-being. How can we reduce or prevent separation anxiety? On the AmDogTraining YouTube channel you can find videos about dogs' stress signals to help you to recognise a state of discomfort in advance, and also how to lower your dog's stress level, encouraging a state of relaxation.

SIX TIPS TO LOWER YOUR DOG'S STRESS LEVEL THAT YOU
CAN USE ON A DAILY BASIS

-Use the blanket

-Promote olfactory research

-Give your dog a relaxing massage

-Provide problem solving games/activities

-Take walks in a peaceful and quiet environment

-Take walks off the lead wherever possible

Don't forget that it could be a good long term investment for
your dog's welfare to seek advice from an expert who can
help you to find the best solutions if you have any problems.
Sometimes a few preventive chats can help you with
managing certain behaviours before they become a problem.

The dog and the blanket

Our busy lives pay little attention to a dog's needs so our pets get placed in stressful situations on a daily basis. Due to lack of time or poor management even the daily walk can become a source of stress.

Our goal must always be the dog's well-being and to achieve this it is paramount that the dog reaches a state of calm.

A very useful gadget that we can use in this respect is the blanket.

We can compare it to a Linus's security blanket, a symbol of indispensable protection.

Studies have proven the benefits of using a specific object during children's development and growth.

It could be a soft toy, a doll or anything else that represents a substitute for a fundamental reference person during their absence. For children at a certain age, this is usually the mother.

The child calms down because they focus on what becomes a sensory transition. The term 'transactional object and/or phenomenon' was first used by the English paediatrician and psychoanalyst Donald Woods Winnicott in the 1940s.

This concept can also be adapted to dogs.

As I usually suggest, when you go to pick a puppy up it is a good idea to also bring home a towel or cloth filled with the smells of the environment where the puppy was born and lived until the moment of adoption.

The towel or cloth will work as an intermediary becoming the first reference point in the new home and, exactly as for children, will represent a transitional experience.

The same principle can be applied to a toy, for example a soft toy from the environment where the puppy was born, which would enable the puppy to emotionally recall that place.

In adult dogs the blanket can become a reference object for relaxation in everyday life and then be used in difficult situations.

HOW TO KEEP YOUR DOG CALM

Most common problems in the relationship between dog and adopter are related to handling difficulties during walks and the dog being easily excitable. Adopters often impose a series of restrictions, while it would be easier and more effective to provide the dog with the necessary support to encourage a state of calm. In this respect the blanket can become the item to help your dog to feel content and relaxed.

WHEN IS IT RECOMMENDED TO USE THE BLANKET?

- In everyday life

- Whenever we move to new environments

- During holidays

- At restaurants

- At boarding kennels or when the dog needs to be separated from us

- In the car

- On any journey by train or plane

- At the vets

- Whenever you feel that your dog needs a 'protected zone'

On several occasions people have been sceptical when I recommended the blanket for adult dogs, but there are no age limits to use tools that promote well-being.

In my many years as a dog lover I have come across trainers who used to keep their dogs in the "down" position for a very long time with the illusion that what they had imposed would get the dogs used to being quiet. It would be as if you were upset and someone tied you up to a chair to help you to relax. This comparison is just to help you understand how an excited dog may feel when asked to lie down for a very long time: it would definitely not be beneficial on their stress level, but would cause even more stress.

HOW TO GET YOUR DOG USED TO THE BLANKET
Choose a quiet place and lay the blanket on the ground.

Sit near the blanket with your dog and enjoy a peaceful and relaxing time together with cuddles and massages.

Separately start teaching your dog to "sit" and "lie-down" so that gradually these positions become a starting point for activities like the feeding ritual and "guna" (you can find all the videos on the YouTube channel that will help you with these).

As a second step, combine relaxation, cuddles or a treat every time the dog approaches the blanket, increasingly waiting for the dog to have direct contact with the blanket.

When you start to see that your dog is naturally approaching the blanket, then repeat the same procedure outdoors as suggested above.

Bring the blanket with you when you go for a trip, or to a restaurant and to any other place where your dog may experience stressful situations. This way you will give your dog a positive emotional feedback that will help them to relax.

To promote the association of blanket=calm you can also place the blanket inside the dog's bed or wherever they experience relaxing situations.

THINGS NOT TO DO

Do not force the dog to stay on the blanket. It must be a choice, not an obligation.

Don't rush it.

Don't ask the dog to "sit" or "lie-down" on the blanket, but prepare these exercises separately.

It may happen that in difficult situations the dog does not feel the need to lie down on the blanket despite it being available. You should leave your dog the freedom to choose.

Do not wash the blanket repeatedly. It is possible to use different blankets, but they will need to get changed allowing odours and scents to be transferred from one to another first.

I am against punishment in any circumstances, but if you are punishing your dog don't do it when the blanket is there. For example, if you decide to lock the dog in the kennel for whatever reason, make sure the blanket is not there to make sure it doesn't get associated with negative emotions.

Now you have all the elements you need to start valuing the "blanket moment" and use transitional experiences in difficult situations!

DIY toys

How can you spend time at home with your best friend?

Here are some problem solving ideas.

When I ask adopters how they play with their dogs the most common answer is "They bring me the ball and I throw it, then I chase them, but they don't let me catch them and sometimes we play tug and pull with the braid."

On the AmDogTraining YouTube channel I have talked about playing in several videos, analysing it from a didactic point of view. Through playing it is possible to learn, communicate, establish rules, roles and social positioning.

I often get asked why even "after playing for an hour, once back home the dog still wants to run and jump".

There is nothing strange about this. Playing with the ball and braid as described above, we 'train' the dog's innate motivation, getting the animal into a loop that stimulates them even more. Chasing a ball and playing tug and pull stimulate the predatory, kinesthetic and possessive motivations so the dog will continue to chase anything that may look like prey, running, moving and feeling that whatever they capture belongs to them. These three motivations are all connected so playing just this way we are only pushing the dog to continually repeat these activities reducing their ability to keep calm.

MENTAL ACTIVATION GAMES

Mental activation games are activities that engage the dog in solving problems, stimulating the acquisition of new cognitive, physical and emotional skills. They encourage training by the use of sight and smell, they promote calmness in helping the dog to manage its emotions, they increase self-esteem and self-efficacy, and they reduce acute stress.

There are various types of such games on the market, varying according to difficulty, material and size. We can also make them ourselves with simple everyday objects, all it takes is a little bit of imagination.

This way, improving communication and working on retrieving we will encourage the dog's cooperation to the detriment of possessiveness, naturally counteracting everything that was amplified through the ball and tug-of-war. The more the dog's brain is trained, the easier it will be for them to solve higher levels of difficulties. Activation games have no contraindications and are suitable for any age, breed and type of behavioural problem because the activity will be "calibrated" according to the individual; moreover, they can be played at home at any time.

In my tutorial I suggest four ideas using common objects for problem solving activities. It is best to start these activities in a quiet environment where disturbances are kept to a minimum.

RULES:

- The dog should learn to stay still during the preparation of the game and start the activity after your "go". This will also work on calmness and self-control.

- Keep short times - avoid continuing if the dog doesn't want to play anymore.

- Increase the level of difficulty proportionately to the dog's abilities.

- The dog must always be able to work out the game on their own. Failure would risk frustration.

- Activities should always be supervised.

- Toys must not put the dog's safety at risk.

- If you have several dogs, activation games should be played individually.

THE SHOEBOX

Using a cardboard shoebox, create a small opening on the long side and place the box upside down (without the lid) on the floor hiding a treat underneath it. The dog, using their muzzle and paws will have to reach the "treasure".

Difficulty: At the beginning, place the treats in front of the opening and then under the box, at this point initially placing the box close to the wall, so that it will be easier for the dog to reach and eat the treat. Moving on to the next level, put the box in the middle of a room with hard flooring and the dog will have to use their paws to prevent it from moving, or they will learn to push it against a wall and reach the treat.

The base of the box can also be used, making it necessary to open the box by "tipping" it with the paws.

THE MAT

A bath mat, which is slightly stiffer than a towel, is used. By rolling it up with treats inside, the dog must unroll it to get the prizes.

Difficulty: the first few times the treats will be within the first few centimetres and then, gradually they will be in the middle. To increase the difficulty, you can also use soft mats or simple towels.

THE FRUIT BOX

Use a wooden fruit box. Place the box upside down and put the treats under the box. The dog should be able to reach them by moving it.

Difficulty: You can hold the box steady with one hand and make sure that the dog has to use their paws to get the treats out. In a second step, a small towel can be placed under the box so that the animal learns to pull the towel with their mouth or paws to get the treats.

THE COLANDER

Use a colander with or without handles. The dog should be able to lift or tip it with their mouth or paws.

Difficulty: The type of floor will make a difference as the colander may start to slide across the room, making it difficult to hold the object in place. Initially you can help your dog by placing something under the edge of the colander so that it can be helped to tip over.

PROPOSING GAMES ACCORDING TO THE DOG'S ABILITIES

Like all the games we usually play with our four-legged friend, mental activation games are also very important for the relationship we build up with our dog. It is essential to propose games suited to their abilities, proceeding step by step and starting with games that are easy to solve, then moving on to more complex ones. It is important to observe and supervise the dog during the activities in order to get to know them better and adapt the games according to their response. As a result, we will improve the dog's skills and we will be more likely to be accredited by our four-legged friend.

Part three

Objectives and activities

The dog: a pacifying animal
Calming signals

Usually, when we talk about training a dog, we refer almost exclusively to giving rules about the correct way to behave in certain situations.

However it is much more effective to concentrate on all the dog's natural characteristics.

Calming signals are cut/break signals, i.e. signals that interrupt aggression and conflict situations.

They began to be discussed in the 1970s in studies about wolves' ethology and two hundred were recognised in wolves and over forty in dogs.

It is important to remember that they are used to:

- prevent the occurrence of events
- avoid threats
- interrupt nervousness, fear and unpleasant situations
- Calming down in situations of stress or discomfort
- transmit tranquillity
- define good intentions in behaviour

They do not necessarily have all these meanings at the same time and it should be remembered that they take on different connotations depending on the context. With reference to a specific problem, several signals may also be present in the same situation.

The main signs are:

- turning the head
- licking the nose
- yawning
- squinting the eyes
- looking elsewhere
- turning sideways and backward
- freezing
- slowing down
- lowering into a playing position
- sitting down, lying down
- sniffing
- following curved trajectories
- wagging the tail
- raising a foreleg
- blinking
- showing indifference

As an example, the first time you put a collar on your puppy they may sit down and freeze . But if you look at it through their eyes, what does that tell you? Surely, considering the neck as a body part with a great social significance, the collar could be seen as a threat.

Consequently in response to a dangerous situation the puppy will use calming signals to:

- avoid a threat
- prevent the occurrence of a potentially dangerous event
- interrupt nervousness, stress and unpleasant situations

Freezing and sitting down, they communicate their state of discomfort and initial difficulty with the unknown collar.

At this point, we have two options in response to the dog's signals: either to stop and take the dog's discomfort into account or to disregard these clear messages and ignore the dog's problems.

Think of the dog saying to you: "Mum, I'm afraid of this torture device you've put around my neck, but what will happen to me now?". Reflect also on the fact that with his biological mother, sitting down and immobilising had always worked to interrupt situations of insecurity.

I could give countless other examples, but the thing I recommend you do is to watch two dogs playing in moments of freedom in a play area and start to interpret all the signals that are part of their communication.

When people say that unfortunately dogs cannot talk I reply

that it would be enough to learn to read all the signals the dog uses to communicate.

Dog's communication is quite simple, if one pays attention to the interaction dynamics and the general context where they take place.

If you fail to interpret a signal used by a dog in an intraspecific conversation, just observe the responses of the other dog.

To help you understand calming signals even better, I recommend you buy this version of the good book: '*Understanding your dog. Calming signals. Twenty-five years later*" by Turid Rugaas, Haqihana Publisher.

On the AmDogTraining website on this subject you can watch the *Area Cani* live broadcast.

Stress signals

Bearing in mind that the dog is a pacifying animal, we can see that in difficult situations the dog expresses their displeasure through calming signals.

For example, imagine that you take your dog to a shopping centre for the first time. There will be noises, lots of people, escalators and many other new things that the dog is unfamiliar with.

From the first moment, through licking, freezing and sometimes sitting, the dog clearly communicates their discomfort and difficulties.

Using the calming signals they are saying: "Mum, this place scares me, what are all these noises? What is happening?".

Leaving aside the fact that you have probably asked a bit too much of them if you haven't introduced the new stimuli gradually, you have now two options: if you pay attention to what the dog is telling you then you can calm the animal down and interrupt the situation that generates discomfort as soon as possible, which is the best thing to do. If, instead, you decide to ignore the signals because you think "They will get used to it!", you will risk turning a simple discomfort into acute stress.

Now, what are the main causes of stress for a dog?

- direct threats from other dogs/humans
- violence and aggression
- being tugged on the lead
- excessive demands during training
- low physical activity
- solitude
- noises
- hot/cold and adverse weather situations
- starvation
- sudden environmental changes
- relaxation difficulties
- pain and illness
- long working times
- too many no's
- relationships based on limitations
- specific needs related to the breed being neglected
- over- excitement
- low excitement

After the calming signals, the dog will again communicate their discomfort through other signals that clearly announce the arrival of a stressful state.

Here is a list of the main stress signals that dogs give:

- nervousness

- restlessness
- excessive reactions (anxiety, fear, aggression...)
- urination and defecation
- licking
- yawning
- piloerection
- wheezing
- biting
- soft faeces
- increased production of mucous from the nose
- fake biting/teeth clicking
- wide-open eyes/shifty eyes
- blinking
- increased sweating from the pads
- biting the lead
- all calming signals
- other individual signals which can be characteristic of that individual.

I would say that at this point it becomes impossible to ignore that something is wrong.

Let's put ourselves in the dog's place once again. It's as if they are saying: "What do I have to do to make you understand that all of this is bothering me? Maybe I could try biting".

In the list of stress signals I have also included all calming signals. One of the questions I am often asked is how I can tell at a particular moment whether the calming signals are really calming signals or whether they should be interpreted as stress signals.

Remember that acute stress can peak within a quarter of an hour.

To help you understand this better, I have made a diagram showing how you get from a difficult situation to an acute stress phase as a timeline:

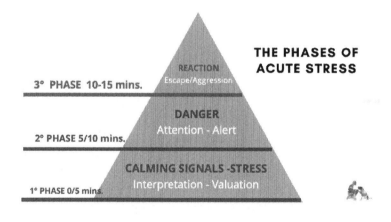

Clearly, as with all tables and graphs, some considerations need to be made.

In this case we are taking time and reactions as a guide only, as there would be other variables to be assessed. But at this moment they are not important to us. The thing that interests us is that within a quarter of an hour it is possible to get to a dog's reaction, as a consequence of stressful situations, and that this reaction can be avoided by paying a little attention.

Conversely, how long does it take to bring the dog back to the initial situation after a quarter of an hour of stress? It may sound strange, but it takes between two and six days, depending on the activities following the stressful event.

At this point I am not saying that it is forbidden to put your dog under stress, but I am suggesting that you limit the moments that put your four-legged companion under stress, preventing them whenever possible and, following unforeseeable ones, look for solutions that can help to reduce tension.

For example, if you are going on a long journey, in the days leading up to it you could try to prepare your dog for an event that will likely be stressful for them: you could, for instance, take walks in quiet surroundings, accompanied by relaxing massages.

In an effort to always provide practical solutions to problems and leave you with suggestions to work on, here are six activities that lower stress in dogs:

- use of the blanket in everyday life
- olfactory research
- relaxing massages

- problem solving activities
- peaceful walks
- walks in complete freedom wherever possible and safe

Motivation in dogs

The International Kennel Federation (FCI) recognises around four hundred breeds and there are more waiting to be considered. It should be pointed out that a standard breed is a fairly accurate description of the physical and behavioural characteristics that an "ideal" subject should possess. The standard is therefore used as a guide and reference for breeders to determine which distinctive traits to favour in selection. The standard also describes the animal in its general appearance, in the details of the individual anatomical parts, also specifying the gait and movement in details.

Also, there can be an innate disposition for certain activities, which becomes particularly important in the evaluation for professional orientation.

Each breed can be genetically different in both appearance and behaviour, so a proper analysis must be made to know the needs of the breed we are dealing with.

Motivation indicates what the dog expects and looks for and can be defined as the combination of need and desire.

"Need" is defined as: "*Any painful sensation arising from present or anticipated dissatisfaction, accompanied by knowledge of the means to lessen, remove or avoid such suffering, and a desire to obtain them*".

And "desire" is *"A feeling of passionate pursuit or expectation of the possession, attainment or implementation of what is felt to be agreeable to one's needs or tastes"*.

THE MAIN MOTIVATIONS:

- predatory: reaching for small moving objects
- territorial: defending a surrounding territory
- protective: defending an associate or a puppy
- scouting: exploring an environment and mapping it
- exploratory: analysing an object in detail
- caring: helping to look after a companion
- receiving care/attention and being happy with it
- searching: looking for hidden objects
- retrieving: collecting objects and carrying them to the den
- courtship: attracting a partner
- affiliative: being part of a small group
- competitive: comparing/competing
- kinesthetic: moving, running or jumping
- somesthetic: exploring one's own body
- collaborative: doing activities with the partner/group
- possessive: maintaining possession of an object
- communicative: expressing a state or indicating something

- social: active search for individuals outside the same group

Outside of what may be a simple list, I would like to try to give you a better understanding of the intrinsic value of motivation, starting with how natural selection has worked.

Here is a slide used during a live event, which you can find in the QR code at the end of the chapter.

In a very basic way: on the left-hand side are the activities that the animal had to carry out for survival and on the right-hand side the motivation that developed as a result of the initial need:

Examples of how a natural selection worked

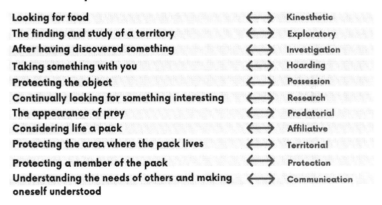

Looking for food	⟷	Kinesthetic
The finding and study of a territory	⟷	Exploratory
After having discovered something	⟷	Investigation
Taking something with you	⟷	Hoarding
Protecting the object	⟷	Possession
Continually looking for something interesting	⟷	Research
The appearance of prey	⟷	Predatorial
Considering life a pack	⟷	Affiliative
Protecting the area where the pack lives	⟷	Territorial
Protecting a member of the pack	⟷	Protection
Understanding the needs of others and making oneself understood	⟷	Communication

In the following table you can see the important change in motivations when he/she becomes part of our daily routine.

Examples of how the home made selection worked

Going for a walk ⟷ Protection-Exploration

Taking something with you ⟷ Hoarding-Possession

Playing with a ball or tug of war ⟷ Kinesthetic-Possession-Predatorial

Boredom ⟷ Research-Investigation

Dog area ⟷ Kinesthetic-Possession-Territorial

Living Together ⟷ Affilliative-Communication

Protecting the area where the dog lives ⟷ Territorial

Considering life in a pack ⟷ Competition

Motivations are present in every dog, but each dog will express them in a different number and way. We should aim to become competent to identify the motivational set that represents our dog, and then to understand how to cope with it.

It should be remembered that there are motivations that feed into others in a positive or negative way. Consequently, the activities we do with our dog every day will be decisive.

I would now like to give some concrete examples to set up a small work programme that can be easily followed.

One of the main problems I get contacted for are over-excited dogs, who do not calm down with physical activity.

Generally the way adopters tend to play with their dogs in these cases, throwing a ball or tug-of-war with a stick or rope, creating loops that self-perpetuate the states of excitement and movement to the detriment of calm and tranquillity.

If you have an excitable dog and you have been playing these games with them, from a motivational point of view you have likely enhanced precisely the kinesthetic, predatory, possessive and sometimes retrieving motivations.

Of all these, the only soft motivation is the syllable one.

Often these games are played in the garden or in the playground, so it takes nothing to increase territorial motivation as well.

By looking at the table below, you can see how some motivations feed into others:

Looking into motivation we must consider that motivation

Favours

COMMUNICATION ←	→ COLLABORATION
COOPERATION ←	→ SOCIALISATION
EPIMELETIC ←	→ ET EPIMELETIC
POSSESSION ←	→ TERRITORIAL
PROTECTION ←	→ AFFILIATIVE
EXPLORATION ←	→ RESEARCH
PREDATORIAL ←	→ KINESTHETIC

If we want to improve the communication with our dog (communicative motivation) our aim will be a cooperative relationship (collaborative motivation).

The table here provides   suggestions on how to set up activities in everyday life.

Looking into motivation we must consider that motivation

Disfavours

PREDATORIAL ← → RESEARCH

TERRITORIAL ← → INVESTIGATION

COMPETITIVENESS ← → COOPERATION

KINESTHETIC ← → COMMUNICATION

POSSESSION ← → HOARDING

PROTECTION ← → SOCIALISATION

These concepts are a bit difficult at first, but once you understand the dynamics, it all becomes very intuitive.

The correct work to be done will always be to rebalance the motivational set. By discouraging stronger motivations in favour of weaker ones, drifts will always be avoided.

Prosociality is the ability of the dog to correctly manage his/her role in social situations. It is necessary, as far as possible, to always favour its development or maintenance (definition of prosociality taken from Roberto Marchesini, *Pedagogia Cinofila, Introduzione all'approccio cognitivo-zooantropologico,* Alberto Perdisa Editore, 2007*).

To make it even simpler, we can define prosociality as the ability of a dog to relate in a correct manner to animals of the same and different species.

In the tables here below you can see the motivations in

relation to prosociality.

MOTIVATIONS THAT UNDERMINE PRO SOCIALITY

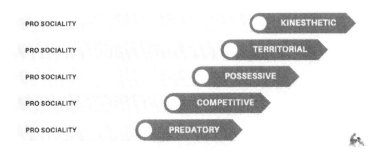

MOTIVATIONS THAT HELP PRO SOCIALITY

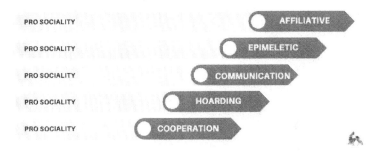

It's not easy to summarise in one chapter such a complicated topic, but my aim is to enable you to understand the probable origin of your difficulties, and then to evaluate alternative solutions and/or to consider expert advice.

Elena Garoni's book *Piacere di conoscerti* (TEA Editore) is remarkable and clearly written, and I absolutely recommend reading it.

An indicator called excitement

With the word "excitement" we refer to the dog's state of emotional activation when responding to internal and external stimuli.

My role in this chapter is to provide you with guidance on how to identify the optimal level of emotional activation of your dog, in order to facilitate learning and reduce an additional source of stress.

The level of excitement is influenced by many variables such as:

- age
- race
- habits
- relationship with the adopter
- social relations
- way of playing
- type of activities proposed

When the excitement is high or low, the dog shows clear difficulties in performing a required task as they are in a state of discomfort.

The goal is an intermediate level of excitement, as it favours interactions and optimises reactions.

In a state of high excitement the dog will show a high state of attention to any surrounding stimulus. This is both good and bad.

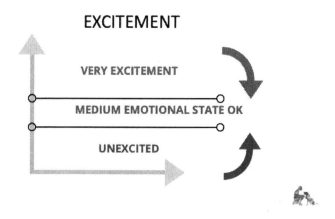

EXCITEMENT

VERY EXCITEMENT

MEDIUM EMOTIONAL STATE OK

UNEXCITED

This state will lead to difficulties in concentrating and will reduce the ability to interact efficiently.

The main signs are restlessness and, indeed, an excessive response to stimuli that will make self-control precarious.

If these "indicators" start to become present, we can bring the dog back to the intermediate level using a simple olfactory search and then mental activation games that enhance cognitive skills.

A simple scent search is just throwing a few treats on the ground for the dog to find them using their sense of smell.

For example, imagine you are out for a walk and your dog becomes restless, pulls on the lead and starts responding to every external stimulus except your requests. When there is no other dog around, throw several tasty treats on the ground at a distance that can be reached staying on the lead, so that the dog starts searching.

This will lower the dog's excitement, make them focus, be calmer and more cooperative again.

In the event that throwing the treats does not bring any results, try to consider that your dog may have been subjected to a very stimulating situation that is difficult to recover from for the time being. If this is the case, remember what happened and next time you should take your dog to a less stimulating environment for a shorter time and introduce activities aimed at attracting your dog's attention. Take the animal's cooperation and response, even if minimal, as indicators.

You will need to provide activities that increase the level of cooperative, communicative, syllable and search motivations. It will be important to accustom your dog to continuous fluctuations in excitement so that they can get used to moving from a high to an intermediate level of excitement within a short time.

To counteract a high level of excitement you will need to intensify any activities that promote the following motivations:

- caring
- receiving care/attention
- collaborative
- communicative
- research

It will be essential to work on calmness, favouring all situations that involve stillness and reduce movement during interaction. Clearly it will be very difficult to obtain positive feedback from the animal if we propose calm activities rather than the level usually used in interaction. This means that we also need to propose any activity in a way that is congenial and stimulating for the dog, and then gradually get to the desired level of calmness.

Don't rush it and work day by day, taking little steps.

Any forms of restraint are not recommended, as they would increase the dog's reactivity and thus their level of excitement.

Dogs with low excitement are apathetic, bored, and have little ability to respond to external stimuli. They are often depressed, with low self-esteem and sometimes show substitution or destruction behaviours. They are uninterested in any activity and even a simple walk would be stressful for them.

It will be necessary to increase the level of predatory, kinesthetic and possessive motivation but there won't be much room for error.

To avoid underestimating problems that are difficult to resolve, when dealing with dogs with low excitement consider consulting qualified people such as dog trainers or veterinary behaviourists who can advise you on how to make any changes in the pet's life.

The motivations that will need to be intensified are:

- kinesthetic
- predatory
- possessive
- communicative
- exploratory

You should be proactive and keep the time very short, trying to encourage novelties and interrupting interactions when your dog is still interested in what you are proposing.

Intermediate excitement: our aim will be to maintain this status as much as possible.

This will provide the dog with the ideal level of concentration to learn and respond to stimuli in an appropriate manner.

In order to make the intermediate excitement a 'lifestyle' for your dog, it is important to recognise and manage the situations that take them away from this comfort zone.

Consider that there may be moments in your dog's day when excitement fluctuates and reaches areas that are difficult to manage. This should be taken as a reference for modifying and adapting activities before and after these moments without necessarily seeing them as a reason for absolute discomfort. Neither low nor high excitement will be a problem as long as they return to the intermediate level within a short time.

Keeping the intermediate level of excitement as a reference will promote the dog's wellbeing and learning process. They will always be ready and pleased to interact with us but will also be able to have a sleep at our side as a source of satisfaction.

This level is promoted by the following motivations:

- collaborative
- searching
- communicative
- retrieving
- receiving care/attention
- caring

The first five exercises to do with a puppy

When it comes to puppies, three categories of new "parents" can be distinguished:

The "Peace-and-love" adopter, the one with no rules and who, in complete adulation, is one hundred per cent available to make any puppy's wish become true. This kind of adopter tends to justify this by saying "They're a puppy anyway, let's hope they'll grow up and settle down". Usually an urgent correction is needed when it becomes difficult to manage the puppy, who is actually no longer a puppy at all.

Dog training programmes should be implemented gradually, as we do with children who start from the nursery and gradually get to university as they grow up.

The "Over-organised" adopter has read books, watched tutorials on the internet, is registered on forums etc., but the problem in this case is that often the puppy becomes forced into facing levels of difficulties which are not appropriate for their age.

On *Il mondo di Olivia (Olivia's world)* playlist, you can find a step by step program that respects the age and abilities of a puppy, in this case Olivia, my own dog.

The "I know!" adopter who is convinced that he/she, having

had dogs since childhood, already has enough experience to be able to proceed.

The fact is that a lot has changed over the years, the role of animals, their space in our lives and our interactions with them have changed.

Whether or not you belong to one of the three categories described, the key point you need to remember is always to look at the world through your dog's eyes and observe their responses as feedback . Adoption is in itself a source of great stress for the puppy, who is forced to change environment and reference figures.

It can take up to a month to get over this stressful phase.

It will be very important for you to recognise the calming and stress signals that the dog uses.

Here are five basic exercises that you can do with a puppy:

EXERCISE 1: GUNA (ALSO CALLED ZEN DOGGY)

Absolutely the first exercise to start with.

Through the Guna, we will encourage the dog to seek our gaze in order to get permission and approval and improve the attention towards us.

Get a treat and hold it in your closed hand, letting the dog smell it, so that they will want to eat it.

Certainly the dog will not remain passive. They will try to get your attention by nibbling at your hand, barking or even jumping. When they realise that their strategy is not effective, they will eventually look at you. At that point, when you get eye contact, you open your hand giving access to the treat.

It is a simple but very important exercise.

This way, in fact, the puppy will learn to look at you as a reference. The puppy will learn that their requests for authorisation are made through eye contact.

EXERCISE 2: SIT

Get a treat and hold it in your hand and check your dog's interest. Bring the hand over the puppy's head and wait for the various possible responses.

They will probably think of jumping and reaching out for your hand in different ways. Stand still and silent, with your hand positioned about twenty to thirty centimetres above their head. When eventually they sit you will open your hand freeing the treat. At a later stage you will also insert a verbal request.

I'm talking about request, not order. If I had suggested starting by using verbal request from the outset, you would have concentrated mainly on intensifying your voice in case of a lack of response from the puppy. This would have been normal for you, because we communicate primarily through speech and just secondarily through proxemics, but it's not the same for a dog.

In parallel, the "sit" position will also be used when giving a meal and will be used to moderate the dog jumping up.

EXERCISE 3: FEEDING TIME

The feeding ritual is a simple and effective way to get accredited by the dog.

The aim is to teach the dog to sit and wait for permission to eat. Also in this exercise we will work on self-control and attention.

Without saying a word, stand in front of the puppy with the bowl in your hands. Stand still. The puppy will of course try different ways to reach the bowl, but without success. When eventually they sit, you lower the bowl to the ground but every time the dog approaches it, you raise it again. The important thing is that the puppy understands that they are not allowed to eat without our permission.

Only later will we introduce the use of a gesture and a verbal "go!", to give access to the food.

We can then begin to lengthen the time and difficulties before giving free access to the bowl. Also in this respect, since we are dealing with puppies, it is a good idea to interrupt the meal from time to time, wait in silence for the dog to sit down again, "top up" the food and allow access to the bowl again. This we will get your dog used to our handling of the bowl and avoid those situations where your dog "growls" during the meal at anyone who approaches or tries to touch the bowl.

EXERCISE 4: RECALLING

Have you ever wondered how recall works amongst dogs?

When a dog wants to recall another to play, they lower themselves on the front paws, turn 180° and then playfully run away to be chased.

Generally you need to behave the same way: so move away, turn your head to the opposite direction and also invite them to join you verbally: "Come on!". As soon as the puppy reaches you, reward them and then - importantly - let them go on to do exactly what they were doing before the recall. This is an "exercise" that must be repeated ten times in around ten-twenty minutes. Only on the ninth time can you can put the lead back on.

Obviously you need to propose this exercise in a safe area.

Usually the recall represents a negative situation because it is perceived as a signal to "end of freedom". It must become something positive, as if the dog thinks: "How nice, you called me, I'll come and get a treat and go back to what I was doing!". You can start building up this exercise at home.

Gradually you will increase the number of disturbances by changing locations.

EXERCISE 5: PLAYING

This is an extensive topic which I have already covered and which you will be able to explore in more detail on the YouTube channel. Toys such as Kong and problem solving games will be preferred.

You can continue to play with balls, sticks and braids - whilst disciplining the activities - and possibly supplementing them with searching. The toys must not always be available to the dog, thus increasing your accreditation.

These five exercises should be offered to your dog on a daily basis, in different contexts and always for a short time, several times during the day.

The puppy must want to work with you and any proposals you make must be seen as a very interesting event. Too much work is perhaps worse than too little work.

It will be good for the puppy to initially have only one person to refer to when constructing the exercises. Only later it should be extended to all family members.

Exercises such as 'guna', 'sit' and 'feed' mainly promote attention and calmness, while recall and playing are dynamic.

I consider the reference to motivation as fundamental in order to be able to understand exactly how each activity should be approached.

And to close this chapter: in case your puppy has difficulties understanding your requests, reflect on the fact that perhaps you have not been clear enough!

Acknowledgements

Reaching the end of a book is a bit like reaching the end of a journey.

Personally, I want to see it as an experience that has been added to my life.

The world is full of books about dogs, but I wanted *my own* book and I want to thank all the people I met in 29 years of dog training. They have contributed to shaping the person I am now and they have shared a part of their life with me.

And, more than anyone else, I'd really like to thank my dogs, both those who have sadly already passed away and those who are still working alongside me in this wonderful adventure: Kettor, Spank, Emi, Teo, Thelma and Olivia. And regarding the two-legged ones, I would like to remember first of all the people who have believed in this project: all the followers who have clicked on the subscribe button on the YouTube channel, helping us to grow day by day.

There are people who come into your life in an apparently random way but you feel like you have known them forever, you find a direct connection with them with simple messages, simple questions and after a possible initial diffidence you realise how easy it is to pursue common goals. In addition to

Nicola, the other half of AmDogTraining, I feel I must add to the thanks Paola Fognani, a person who has been fundamental in the writing of the book.

One thing leads to another and everything has its own karma. She was enthusiastic about our project.

Faced with an immense amount of material, she managed to unravel the skein in record time, handling many editorial aspects of our work with infinite patience, sharing her expertise with us.

As I wrote this evening in a message to Nicola, I owe the last few amazing months to them. In different ways, they have allowed me to go through this experience, relieving me from the burden of extremely important tasks and, at the same time, allowing me to carry out my role even though I was beginning to feel the fatigue.

In fact, I feel happy, because being able to write a book represented a dream for me, something I would have never imagined that could have become possible until just recently. I was already proud of the collaboration I had achieved with Quattro Zampe magazine. And in this regard, I would like to thank MP, as I usually call her, Maria Paola Gianni, head of Quattro Zampe, and the director of Edizioni Morelli, Giovanni Morelli, for their trust since the very beginning. I would like to thank Mario Neri and his staff at Studio Latte+ for creating the splendid book cover.

I sincerely thank Julie Renwick for her contribution to this book.

And we really do come to the end.

Last but not least, I would like to thank my two children Ele and Manu, my wife Elisa, my parents and my brother, who have often seen me running, fugitive and elusive in favour of a dog-loving activity that today has led me to write a book: my book!

Bibliography

The bibliography about dogs is truly immense. I will limit myself here by indicating those publications that seem paramount considering the topic addressed in this book.

Alquati. P., *Character tests for young dogs*, Edizioni Cinque, 1992

Barbieri I., *Lezioni di cinognostica*, Edizioni ENCI, 1975

Behan K., *Your dog is your mirror. True friendship, identical emotions*, De Vecchi Editore, 2015

Bonetti F., *Zoognostica del cane*, Editrice San Giorgio, 1995

Colangeli R., Giussani S., *Behavioural medicine of dogs and cats*, Poletto Editore, 2004

Coren S., *The Intelligence of Dogs*, Oscar Mondadori Essays, 1996

Coren S., *Understanding the language of dogs*, Franco Muzzio Editore, 2003

De Martini G.C, De Martini C., *Addestra il tuo cane*, Sonzogno, 1996

Desachy F., *I problemi comportamentali del cane*, De Vecchi Editore, 2000

Desachy F., *The puppy. Breeding - education. Things to know*, De Vecchi Editore, 2000

Dodman N. H., *The dog who loved too much. Behaviour and psychology of the dog*, Longanesi, 1997

Dodman N. H., *If only they could talk*, Longanesi & C., 2003

Fennell J., *Ascolta il tuo cane*, Salani Editore, 2002

Fennell J., *Sai comunicane?*, Salani Editore, 2004

Fisher J., *Why does my dog do that?* Alberto Perdisa Editore, 2004

Gallicchio B., *Lupi transvestiti. Le origini biologiche del cane domestico*, Edizioni Cinque, 2009

Garoni E., *Piacere di conoscerti*, Tea Edizioni, 2019

Kvam A. L. *The dog's sense of smell between play and work*, Haqihana Publishing, 2007

Lorenz K., *And Man Met the Dog*, Adelphi Edizioni, 1974

Lorenz K., *King Solomon's Ring*, Adelphi Edizioni, 1989

Mann T., *Master and Dog*, Biblioteca Universale Rizzoli, 1954

Marchesini R., *Animali di città*, Red Edizioni, 1997

Marchesini R., *Canone di zooantropologia applicata*, Alberto Perdisa Editore, 2004

Marchesini R. *A lezione dal mondo animale*, Alberto Perdisa Editore, 2004

Marchesini R., *Bastardo a chi?*, Fabbri Editore, 2007

Marchesini R., *Pedagogia cinofila. Introduction to the cognitive zooanthropological approach*, Alberto Perdisa Editore, 2013

Marchesini R., *Pet Therapy. Practical manual*, De Vecchi Editore, 2015

Mayer C., Dog *Fitness. Your dog in* shape, Macro Editions, 2018

Meneghetti V., *Manual of modern applied psychology*, Edizioni Cinque, 1998

Morris D., *The dog. All the whys*, Oscar Mondadori, 1998.

Nagel M., v. Reinhardt C., *Stress in the dog*, Haqihana Publisher, 2020

O'Farrell V., *Dog Behaviour and Psychology*, Oscar Mondadori, 1991

Overall K. L., *The behavioural clinic of the dog and cat*, C. G. Edizioni Medico Scientifiche, 2001

Pageat P., *Behavioural pathology of the dog*, PVI, 1999

Polverini L., *Dalle parole ai fatti. Dal perché fare al come fare*, Edizioni Altea, 2010

Pryor K., *Training with the clicker*, ERA ORA Editions, 2006

Rossi V. *Guida completa all'addestramento del cane*, De Vecchi Editore, 1991

Rossi V., *Understanding the language of the dog*, De Vecchi Editore, 2017

Rowlands M., *The wolf and the philosopher. Life lessons from the wild*, 2017 Mondadori

Rugaas T., *Help my dog pull!*, Haqihana Publisher, 2004

Rugaas T., *Understanding with dogs. Calming signals*, Haqihana Publisher, 2005.

Sims G., *The Dog Whisperer*, De Agostini, 2012

Sims G., *The Secret Language of Dogs*, Sperling & Kupfer, 2014

Solaro G. *Sunto delle lezioni di zoognostica canina,* Edizioni Enci, 1958

Trumler E. Face to *face with the dog*, Orme Edizioni, 2011

Index

Part 3. *Objectives and insights*

Printed in Poland
by Amazon Fulfillment
Poland Sp. z o.o., Wrocław

87002510R00076